Wiltrud Roser

LENA and LEOPOLD

Translated from the German by Elizabeth D. Crawford

PUFFIN BOOKS

PUFFIN BOOKS
Published by the Penguin Group
Viking Penguin Inc., 40 West 23rd Street, New York, New York 10010, U.S.A.
Penguin Books Ltd, 27 Wrights Lane, London W8 5TZ England
Penguin Books Australia Ltd, Ringwood, Victoria, Australia
Penguin Books Canada Ltd, 2801 John Street, Markham, Ontario, Canada L3R 1B4
Penguin Books (N.Z.) Ltd, 182–190 Wairau Road, Auckland 10, New Zealand

Penguin Books Ltd, Registered Offices: Harmondsworth, Middlesex, England

First published in Switzerland by Atlantis Kinderbücher/Verlag Pro Juventute, 1985
First published in the United States of America
by Margaret K. McElderry Books/Macmillan Publishing Company, 1987
Published in Picture Puffins 1988
1 3 5 7 9 10 8 6 4 2
Copyright © Verlag Pro Juventute, Zurich, 1985
Translation copyright © Elizabeth D. Crawford, 1987
All rights reserved
Printed in Hong Kong by South China Printing Company
Set in Garamond #3

Library of Congress Cataloging in Publication Data
Roser, Wiltrud.
[Lena und Leopold sein gute Freunde, aber—English]
Lena and Leopold/Wiltrud Roser; translated from the German by Elizabeth D. Crawford.
p. cm.—(Picture puffins)
Translation of Lena und Leopold sein gute Freunde, aber—.
Summary: Lena finally finds out why her cat Leopold won't play with his new toy mouse.
ISBN 0-14-050818-X   [1. Cats—Fiction.]   I. Title. [PZ.R71954Le 1988]   [E]—dc19   88-11704

LENA and LEOPOLD

Lena and Leopold are good friends,
but after Lena's birthday they quarreled almost every day!

"Why can't we play with my birthday mouse?" Lena would ask.
"Because her ears are too big," Leopold said one time.
Another time he said, "Because her tail is too thin."
All the same, Lena thought it was the most beautiful toy mouse
in the whole world.

One day Lena didn't come out to play.
She was lying in bed in broad daylight.
"Are you sick?" asked Leopold.
"A little," said Lena.
"Can I do something for you so that
you'll be well again soon and can play with me?"
"You can eat up my bread and jam."

Leopold shoved the plate of bread away,
all the way down to the end of the bed.
He couldn't stand gooseberry jam.
"I'd rather tell you about my friend Bobo,
who was sick too, once, and didn't want anything to eat."

Bobo

Isidor Annabelle Pompador Pimpernel

Bobo was still a very young cat then.
He was much bigger and stronger and wilder
than his brothers and sisters, Isidor and Annabelle,
Pompador and Pimpernel.
His mother was proud of him.

"My dear Bobo," said she
whenever she was going out—and she went out often—
"my dear Bobo, look after our little ones.
I'll bring back something nice for all of you."
"My dear Mama Mitzi," said Bobo,
"don't worry, but bring us a lot of something nice when you come back."

Mama Mitzi was scarcely out of the house when Bobo,
along with Isidor and Annabelle, Pompador and Pimpernel,
went into the kitchen.
"Now, be good and sit at the cat table and watch me,"
Bobo said. "I'll just eat up this horrible kitten food
and then I'll go into the pantry and get something better for you."

But Bobo ate the something better all by himself, too. And
all the while he complained, "The cream is too rich, the
sausage is too spicy, the cake is too sweet, the pudding is
too cold. This is no food for little kittens. Instead, let me show you
what I can do."

Bobo was the biggest and fastest doll-ripper

and the best dish-smasher of them all.

Bobo thought up the most wonderful games.
But just when it was getting to be the most fun, he would disappear.

And he was never anywhere to be found when Mama Mitzi came home and handed out spankings.

From early to late Isidor and Annabelle,
Pompador and Pimpernel complained about their big brother.

But when Mama Mitzi went out to the cat concert at night,
the little ones were glad that Bobo was big and strong
and wild and took good care of them.

Once Mama Mitzi came home a little earlier than usual
and waked her children.
"Just look at what ran across my path today,"
she said. "A white mouse with a little pink
tail! Never have I seen such a nice little mouse.
I want to keep this one. Don't hurt it!"

Mama Mitzi stayed home the whole day
and they played cat and mouse.

Then, suddenly, the nice little mouse was gone.
Mama Mitzi looked sharply at her children,
one after the other. Bobo was last.

Bobo grinned.
A little pink tail hung out of his mouth.
I'd better get out of here, he thought, and
stood up.
And then the mouse slipped down into his tummy!
It was just terrible.

Isidor and Annabelle, Pompador and Pimpernel
laughed themselves silly over Bobo's wild
jumps and funny faces.
They ate themselves full of kitten food
and felt big and strong.
It was a wonderful day.

But at night they were helpless little kittens again.
"A flea is biting me," howled Isidor. "I'm afraid,"
wailed Annabelle. "Mama Mitzi, don't leave us. We love you!"
whimpered Pompador and Pimpernel.

All the excitement was good for Bobo.
His dreadful stomachache felt a little better.
"Just go, Mama Mitzi," he groaned.
"Go to your cat concert. I'll take care of them."

The next day Bobo was still very sick.
He just wanted to rest. Anyone who has ever swallowed a
whole mouse would understand that.
But Isidor and Annabelle, Pompador and Pimpernel whined,
"Bobo has to get up! Bobo has to play with us!
What shall we do without Bobo?"
"Be nice to Bobo," said Mama Mitzi.
"Then he'll get well again soon."

Isidor and Annabelle, Pompador and Pimpernel were very nice.
They even got Bobo's favorite food out of the pantry.
That made him feel even sicker.

Each day they stole more out of the pantry.
They got bigger and bigger and stronger and stronger,
and Bobo got worse and worse.

On the fifth day Bobo hid under the comforter
and wouldn't come out.
Isidor and Annabelle, Pompador and Pimpernel
howled so loud that they could be heard out in the street.
"What's going on here?" asked old Higgettyhodge.
"Bobo doesn't want any whipped cream or chocolate cake
or lemon ice or strawberry ice cream!"
"Phooey!" exclaimed old Higgettyhodge,
"that's no food for a wild tomcat!
I know what he needs."

And he presented Bobo
with a big fat gray mouse.

Then Bobo sprang out of bed and ran through the
house, crying, "No, no! I will never, never, ever,
ever eat another mouse again!"

The story was over,
and a mouse was nibbling Lena's bread and jam.
But where was Leopold?
Under the covers! Do you see him?

"Dear Leopold," said Lena, laughing,
"admit it, your friend Bobo is you!
Now I know: the sight of any mouse makes you sick,
so I'll put my birthday mouse in the closet and
never take her out again."